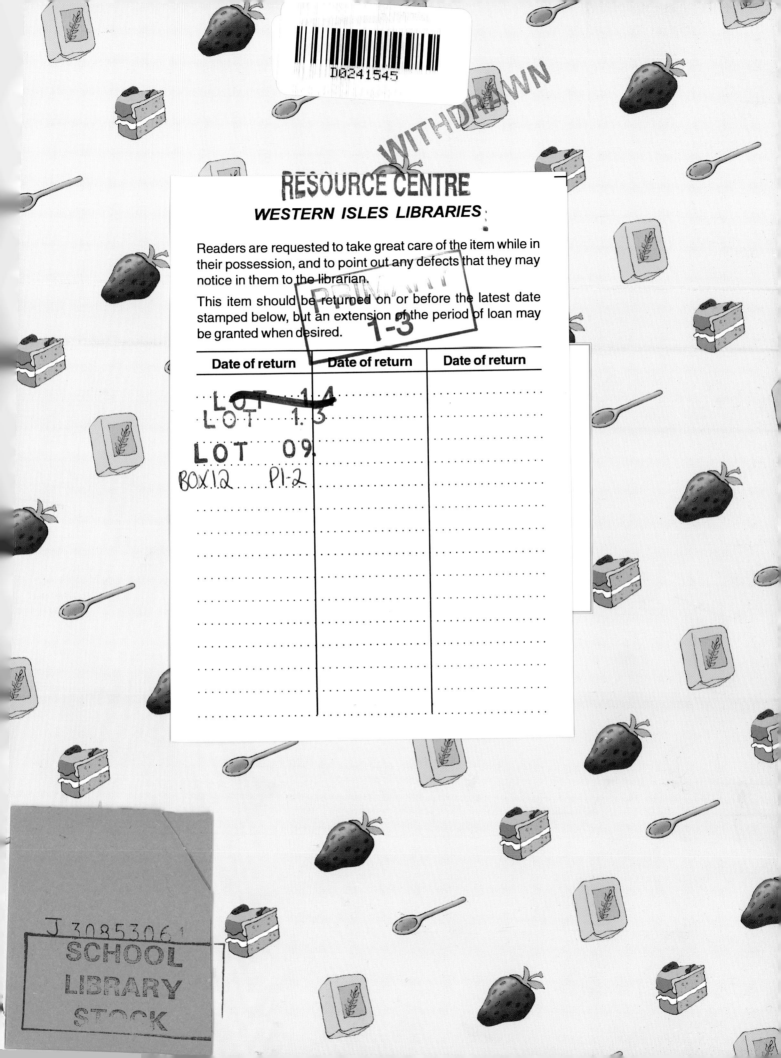

Meet the Large family

Mr Large

Mr Large does his best to help out around the house and manages to stay calm amid the chaos created by his boisterous children.

Lester Large

Nine-year-old Lester just wants to look cool and play on his skateboard. He loves his family, but often finds them a bit embarrassing.

Luke Large

Luke is cheerful and sometimes shy. He looks up to his cool older brother Lester, but still enjoys playing with his toys, especially his old favourite, Mr Teddy.

Mrs Large

Mrs Large is always in a rush as she struggles to cope with her four children and mountains of washing. But she always has time to join in the fun!

Laura Large

Helpful and good-natured, Laura is a caring big sister to baby Lucy. She is creative and practical and enjoys making things.

Lucy Large

Lucy is the baby of the family. She gets into mischief the moment Mrs Large turns her back and her naughty little trunk finds its way into everything.

First published 2008 by Walker Books Ltd
87 Vauxhall Walk, London SE11 5HJ

2 4 6 8 10 9 7 5 3 1

Copyright © 2008 Coolabi, Go-N Productions, Luxanimation & DQ Entertainment
Based on the animation series THE LARGE FAMILY by JILL MURPHY
Developed and produced by Coolabi and Go-N Productions (France)
in association with Luxanimation and DQ Entertainment

The right of Jill Murphy to be identified as the author and artist of this work has been
asserted by her in accordance with the Copyright, Designs and Patents Act 1988.

This book has been typeset in Bembo Educational.

Printed in China

British Library Cataloguing in Publication Data: a catalogue record for this book
is available from the British Library

ISBN 978-1-4063-1473-1

www.walkerbooks.co.uk

Laura Bakes
a Cake

Based on the Large Family stories by Jill Murphy

WALKER BOOKS
AND SUBSIDIARIES
LONDON • BOSTON • SYDNEY • AUCKLAND

Mrs Large and Lucy were shopping at Mr Short's supermarket.

"Oh no, you don't!" said Mrs Large, as Lucy
helped herself to a bar of chocolate.

Mrs Large took the chocolate from Lucy's trunk
and put it back on the shelf.

"The sooner we're out of here the better," she
said.

Mr Short was admiring the large pyramid of cans he had just built, when Mrs Large and Lucy came round the corner.

By now Lucy was tired of sitting in the trolley,
so she stood up and flung her arms around her
mother's neck. The trolley pushed away behind
her and hurtled towards the cans.
CRASH! Cans flew in all directions.
"Oh no!" gasped Mrs Large.

"If we're not careful, Mr Short won't let us come into his shop any more." Mrs Large told Lucy, when they got home.

While her mother was busy making a cup of tea, Lucy opened the bag of flour that they had just bought.

Mrs Large turned around and saw Lucy, covered
in flour from trunk to toe.
"Oh, Lucy!" she cried. "Not the flour!"
Lucy sneezed. "AH-TISHOO!"

Laura was very excited when Mrs Large
arrived to pick the children up from school that
afternoon.
"We're going to make a strawberry jam sponge
cake tomorrow!" she said.

As they walked home, Lucy got hold of Mrs Large's handbag when no one was looking and took out her mother's purse . . .

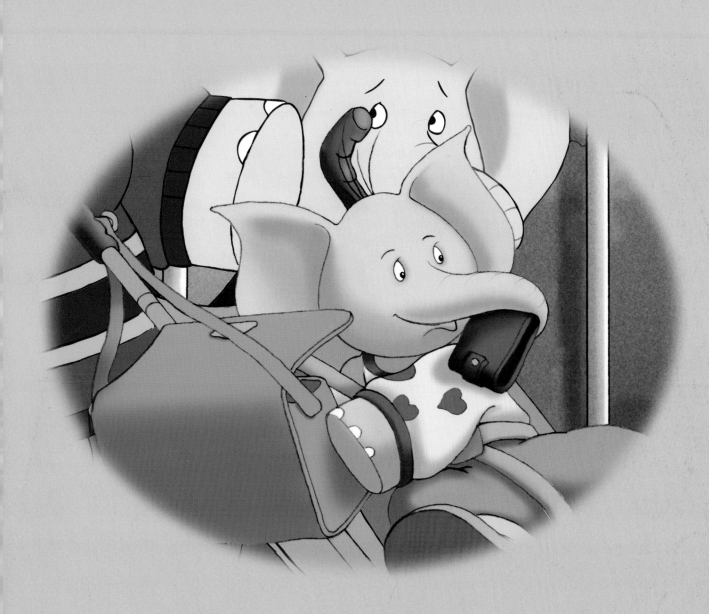

"I'm cooking a cake at school tomorrow," Laura told everyone that evening, "and I need to take some flour."

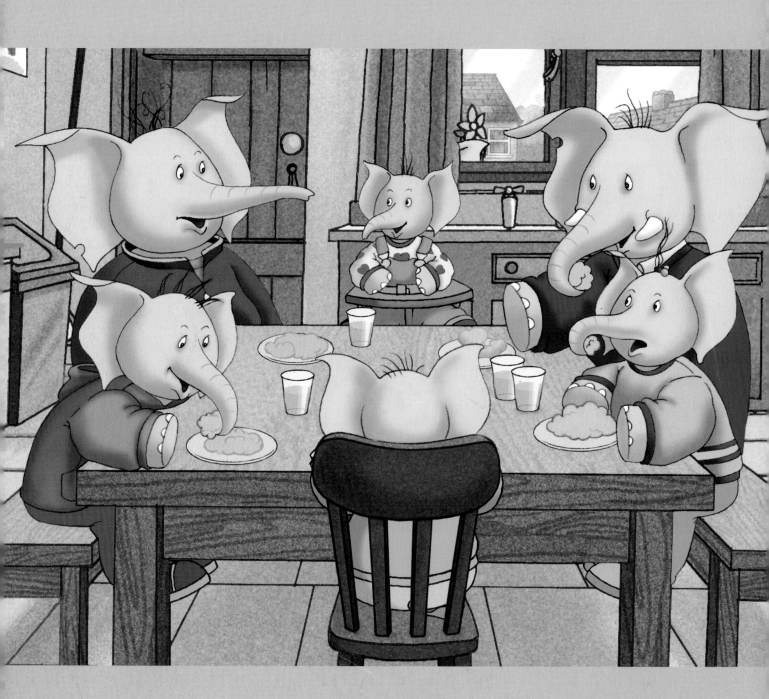

"Don't talk to *me* about flour . . ." Mrs Large
groaned.
"But I've got to have some for school
tomorrow," said Laura.
"Why on earth didn't you tell me earlier?" cried
Mrs Large.

Mrs Large and Laura dashed out of the front door. They hadn't gone far when Mrs Large opened her bag and saw that her purse was missing.

They raced back to search for it.
Mrs Large looked in the bath, while Laura
peered inside the washing machine.

Lester lifted up
the cushions,
while Mr Large
looked in the
fridge.

Finally Luke
found it under the
pushchair.

Mr Short was closing his shop by the time they
arrived.
"Wait –" gasped Mrs Large.
"Too late!" said Mr Short.

"But all we need is one bag of flour," pleaded Laura. "It's for my school cake!"
Mr Short took no notice and carried on pulling down the shutters.
"What are we going to do now?" cried Laura.

On the way home, Mrs Large had an idea. They could ask their neighbour, Mrs Smart, if Sebastian would share his flour with Laura. Sebastian agreed immediately. "No problem," he said cheerfully.

"But we've only got enough for one cake!" Mrs Smart said sharply. "In *our* house, we always make a shopping list so we don't forget things!"

Laura looked miserable as they set off for school the next day.

Sebastian came out with his cake ingredients in a basket.

While they were chatting, Lucy slid her trunk into the basket. She took out an egg and smashed it on the pavement. Then another.

"Stop her!" screamed Mrs Smart.

But Lucy already had the third egg in her trunk – and she was aiming it at Mrs Smart's car!

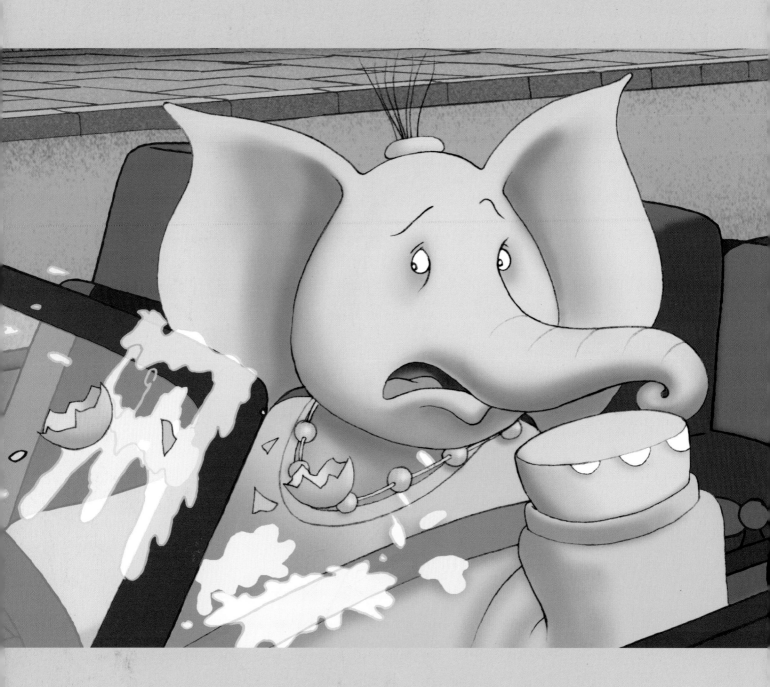

"Oh *really*!" Mrs Smart snorted. "My new blouse
– and how can Sebastian make the best sponge
in the class without any eggs?"

"Don't worry," Laura said, "we've got loads."

"Well then," announced Mrs Smart, "you must share them with Sebastian."

"Does that mean I can share my flour?" Sebastian asked.

"I *told* you, Sebastian," his mother insisted, "there's only enough for one cake."

"Then we'll make one cake *together*!" said Sebastian happily.

Laura and Sebastian came out of school,
carefully carrying a beautiful strawberry jam
sponge cake.
"It looks fantastic!" said Mrs Large.

"I can see which half is yours, Sebastian," said
Mrs Smart proudly. "It's that one, isn't it? It looks
so much lighter and fluffier!"

That evening, the Large family all enjoyed a slice of the strawberry jam sponge.

"What do you think?" Laura asked anxiously.
"We think it's the most delicious strawberry
sponge cake we've ever tasted!" her mother said.
"In fact, Laura, you can bake all the cakes from
now on!"

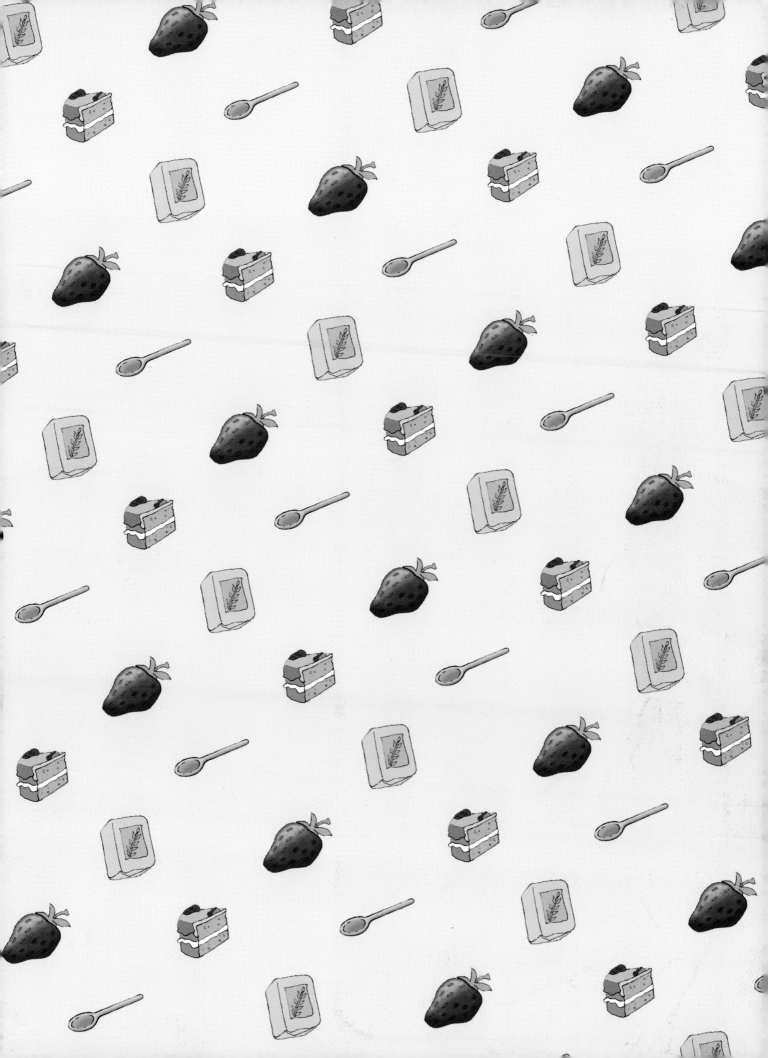